For my children with thanks –
K.H.

For Brady Jane –
T.K.

First published 1999 by Walker Books Ltd
87 Vauxhall Walk, London SE11 5HJ

This edition published 2000

10 9 8 7 6 5 4 3 2 1

Text © 1999 Kathy Henderson
Illustrations © 1999 Tony Kerins

This book has been typeset in Weiss.

Printed in Hong Kong

British Library Cataloguing in Publication Data
A catalogue record for this book is
available from the British Library.

ISBN 0-7445-6360-7

The
BABY DANCES

Kathy Henderson

illustrated by
Tony Kerins

WALKER BOOKS
AND SUBSIDIARIES
LONDON · BOSTON · SYDNEY

The baby's born.
The baby's born.

In the middle of winter

and a windy, rattling, late rainstorm

she has her first warm hug

in her father's arms …

look, the baby's born!

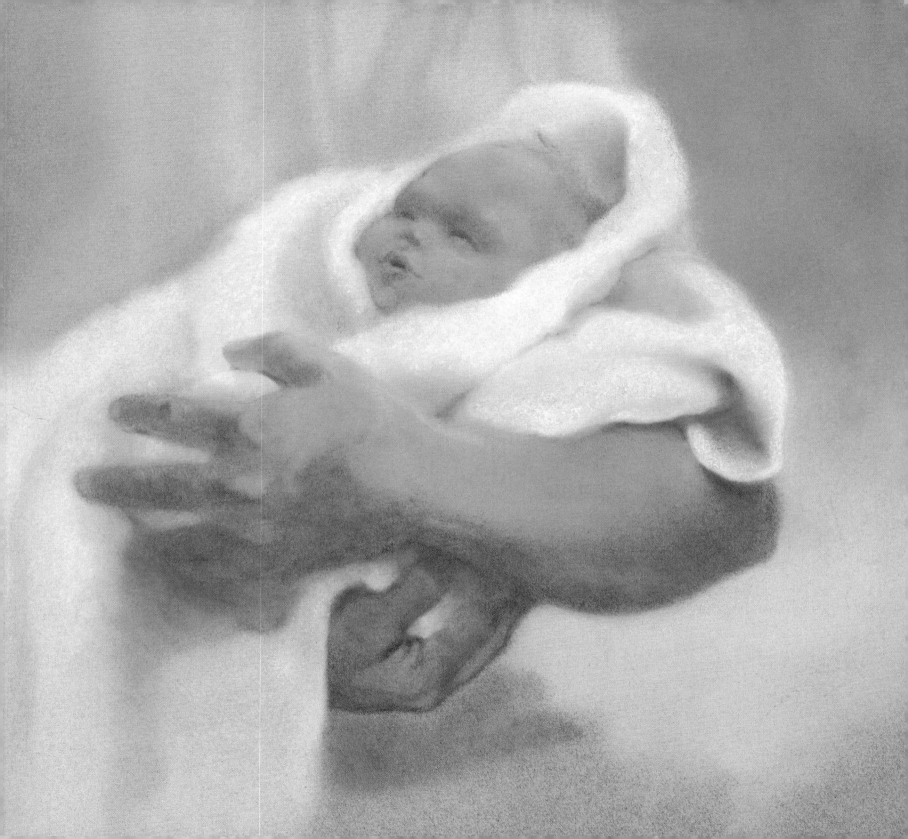

The baby sleeps.
The baby sleeps.

And the pale sun reaches

the windowsill,

where everything is still

in a room full of flowers,

and the baby sleeps for hours.

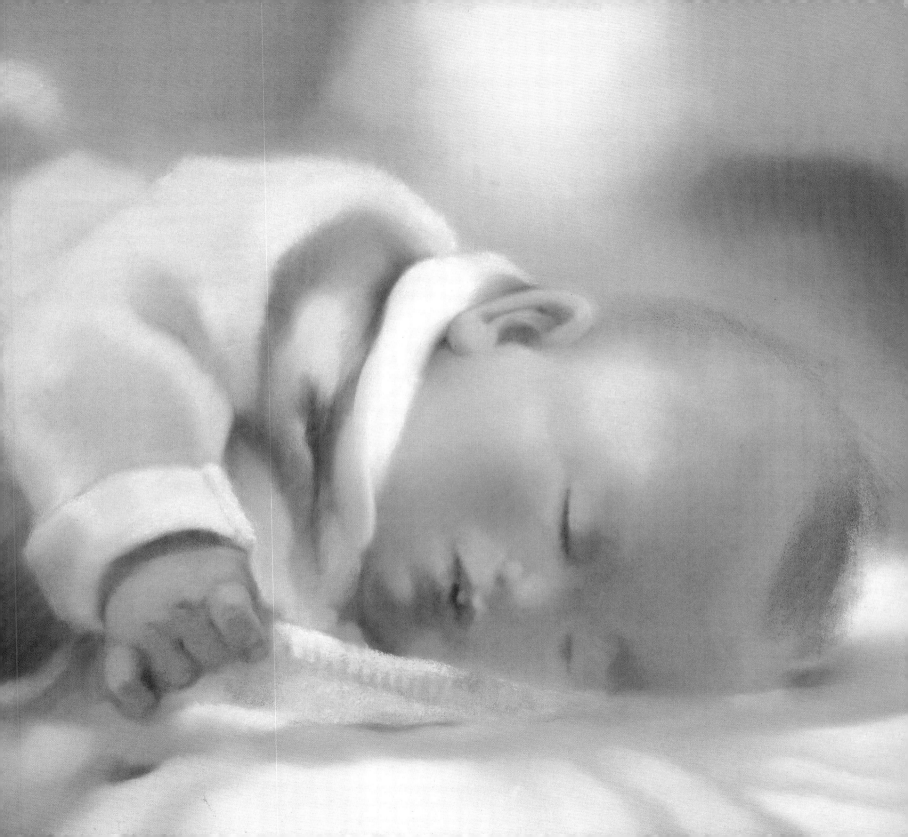

The baby's smiling.
The baby's smiling.

Lying on her back

with the spring sun shining,

riding by the blossom

and the faces passing,

now the baby's smiling.

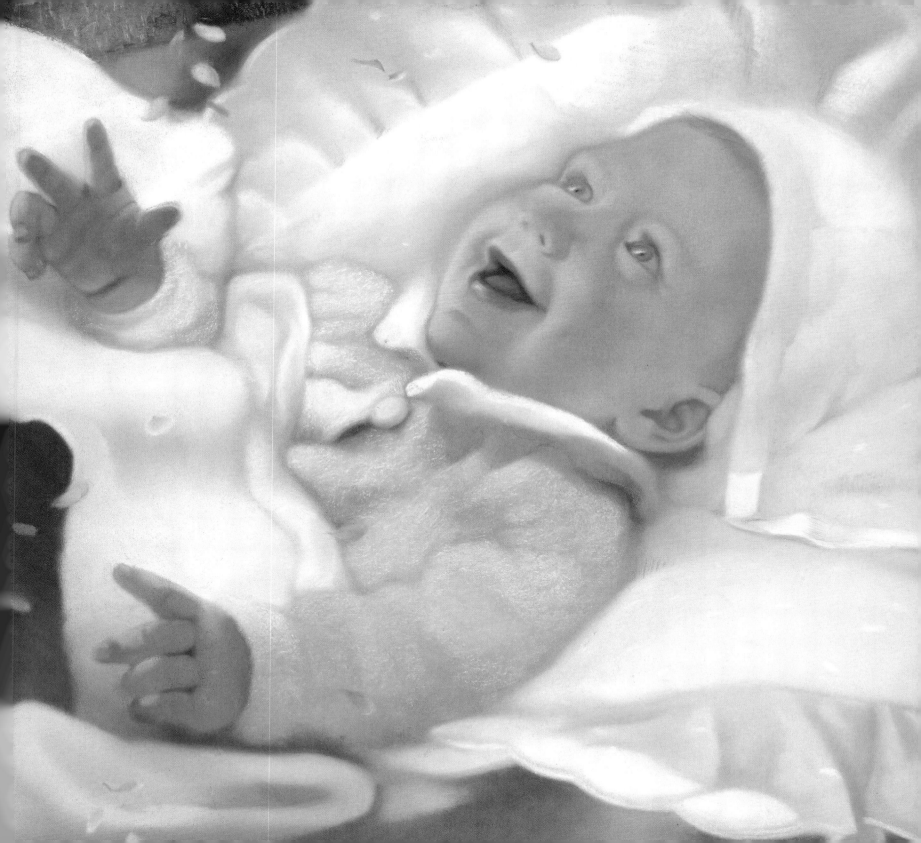

The baby rolls.
The baby rolls.

On her rug in the grass

she tips the whole world up,

with a kick and a wriggle

and a handful of clover …

the baby rolls herself over.

The baby sits.
The baby sits

with a cushion there to catch her

'cause she sways and leans

and wobbles a bit,

and she waves her hands at shadows

and her sunhat tips

but the baby sits.

The baby crawls.
The baby crawls.

From sprawling on the rug

now she rocks on all fours,

and reaching out her hand

as the first dry leaf

of autumn falls …

the baby crawls.

The baby stands.
The baby stands

like a tightrope walker

in the gusty wind,

for a long split second

she lifts her hands,

and all on her own

the baby stands.

The baby walks.
The baby walks.

In the warm by the fire

while the winter beats outside,

she takes her first lurching steps

reaches out …

staggers … prances …

and safe in her brother's arms,

the baby dances!

WALKER BOOKS

The Baby Dances

KATHY HENDERSON says that *The Baby Dances* was a special text for her. "I wrote it as a celebration of my own children and all babies, of the natural world and the extraordinary gift of being alive. Maybe it's also a sort of guide to the first year of life. If you've got a little baby in your household, as sure as spring follows winter and summer follows spring, you're going to witness the most amazing bit of growing and learning any of us ever do, as amazing as the way leaves grow on the trees."

Kathy Henderson has written many acclaimed stories for children. Her picture books include *Fifteen Ways to Go to Bed* (shortlisted for the Smarties Book Prize); *In the Middle of the Night*; *The Little Boat* (Winner of the Kurt Maschler Award and shortlisted for the Smarties Book Prize); *The Year in the City* (Winner of

the 'Primary Education' Book Award) and *The Storm*. She has three children and lives in north London.

TONY KERINS says that "on a personal level *The Baby Dances* is very special. When I started the illustration, my own son had just turned one. I had witnessed a year filled from day to day with exciting little changes. It was such a rich experience. I wanted each picture in the book to show the emotion of the moment of change."

Tony Kerins has illustrated numerous books for children. He also teaches drawing and illustration, designs stage sets and exhibits his drawings. He is the author and illustrator of two titles for Walker Books, *The Brave Ones* and *Little Clancy's New Drum*. He has five children and lives in Swanage.

ISBN 0-7445-5253-2 (pb)

ISBN 0-7445-5460-8 (pb)

ISBN 0-7445-5283-4 (pb)

ISBN 0-7445-6042-X (pb)

ISBN 0-7445-3143-8 (pb)